PUPPY PATROL ™

THE SEA DOG

BOOKS IN THE 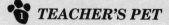 PUPPY PATROL SERIES ™

COMING SOON

PUPPY PATROL ™

THE SEA DOG

JENNY DALE

Illustrations by Mick Reid
Cover illustration by Michael Rowe

AN
APPLE
PAPERBACK

SCHOLASTIC INC.
New York Toronto London Auckland Sydney
Mexico City New Delhi Hong Kong Buenos Aires

SPECIAL THANKS TO MARY HOOPER

No part of this publication may be reproduced in whole or in part, or stored in a retrieval system, or transmitted in any form, or by any means, electronic, mechanical, photocopying, recording, or otherwise, without written permission of the publisher. For information regarding permission, write to Macmillan Publishers Ltd., 25 Eccleston Place, London SW1W 9NF and Basingstoke.

ISBN 0-439-21814-4

12 11 10 9 8 7 6 5   3 4 5 6/0

Printed in the U.S.A.   40
First Scholastic printing, October 2001

CHAPTER ONE

Neil Parker stirred under the unfamiliar sheets and blankets on his bed and groped for a nonexistent comforter.

Outside his bedroom window, there was a howling sound; a mournful, sorrowful cry from an animal in distress.

"What's up?" he muttered, half asleep. "What do you want?"

Then suddenly he was wide awake.

For a moment, Neil was disoriented. Where was he? The clouds outside the window moved and a shaft of moonlight fell into the room. He blinked. Of course! He wasn't in his home at King Street Kennels — it was spring break and the whole Parker family was on vacation in Cornwall. Neil's Uncle Jack and Kate, the kennel assistant, were looking after the dog kennels and rescue center that the Parkers ran in Compton, near Manchester.

Neil lifted his head and strained to listen. There really *was* a dog howling outside; he hadn't been dreaming. He sat up and looked toward the other bed in the room. At home he had a bedroom to himself, but the vacation cottage was so tiny, he had to share with his nine-year-old sister Emily. His other sister, five-year-old Sarah, was in a bed in their mom and dad's room.

"Emily!" he called over in a hoarse whisper. "Are you awake?"

There was no reply.

"Emily!"

Outside, the dog continued to howl.

Surely it couldn't be Sam, his black-and-white Border collie. Even if he'd gotten stuck outside in the cold, Sam would never howl like that!

Neil slid out of bed. Quietly, he crept downstairs and pushed open the door that led into the cozy sitting room of the cottage, which was crammed with comfy sofas and armchairs. In the gloom, Neil could just make out the low ceiling and the dark beams running along the length of the room. Around the walls were various old prints and photographs of boats. On the mantelpiece there was a ship in a bottle, and various brass instruments which, Neil supposed, originally came from ships.

No, it was all right — Sam was still lying where Neil had left him, curled up on an old blanket in front of the dying embers of the fire.

Sensing Neil's presence, Sam jumped up and ran over to him. He was excited to see Neil at such a strange hour and was instantly ready to play.

"Calm down, Sam. Calm down," Neil said, speaking softly and scratching the soft fluffy fur around the dog's ears.

The collie looked at him eagerly, his brown eyes alert for whatever was coming. "No, we're not going out," Neil went on, "I just wanted to make sure that you were all right."

Neil turned sharply toward the window. The howling came again from outside, louder and more insistent.

"There it is again. Now, what do you think that is, Sam?" he asked. Sam tilted his head to one side, as if considering the question, and gave a little whine.

Neil sighed. He knew he'd never go back to sleep now, not when he knew that somewhere outside was a dog in distress.

"Lie down, Sam," he said. "I'm just going out to have a quick look around."

Neil tiptoed back to his bedroom, pulled on his jeans and a sweatshirt, and put on his sneakers.

"I won't be long!" he whispered to Emily. "I'm going out to find a dog."

Emily didn't reply. She just murmured something in her sleep.

Downstairs, it was clear that Sam expected to come with him. Before Neil had crossed the room, the collie was waiting at the back door in the kitchen.

"No, Sam, I don't want you outside in the cold," Neil said to him softly. "You're supposed to be down here to recuperate. You need lots of rest and relaxation." Sam's life at King Street Kennels had been just a bit too eventful lately. He'd been diagnosed with a heart murmur and had been very sick. After a lot of worrying by the Parkers, Sam was back to his old self, but he still had to take it easy. And now his girlfriend, Delilah, had given birth to Sam's puppies — and one of them would be coming to live with Neil when it was big enough. Sam had really had enough excitement.

Sam gave a soft bark.

"Sssh!" Neil said. "I don't want to wake anyone up." Gently, he pushed Sam back from the door. He unbolted the door and lifted the latch to let himself out. "I won't be long. I just want to find out what's going on."

The Parkers' vacation home was a small stone cottage called Summerbreeze. It stood high on the cliffs above the little fishing village of Tregarth. In front of the cottage was a stony, bumpy road lined with a few windblown trees and bushes. Through the gate and to the right, the road led down to the village and the small harbor. It forked off halfway down to go along the cliff toward a wharf that jutted into the sea.

Neil stood outside the door in the night air, waiting to hear the dog howl again so he'd know which way to go. The moon suddenly went behind a cloud so that Neil could barely see his hand in front of him. The branches of a nearby tree swayed with a loud creaking noise, making him jump.

He rubbed his arms to keep warm and listened intently, half hoping that the dog wouldn't howl again and that he could go back to his warm bed.

But the howl did come once more, low and mournful, somewhere to his right. Neil took a deep breath and set off down the deserted road.

Although the moon was still obscured by clouds, Neil's eyes grew accustomed to the dark quickly. He wished Sam had been able to come with him; a dog's senses were so much more acute. Sam would be able to seek out a dog in trouble in no time.

Neil strained to see ahead and make sense of the landscape. Everything about it was strange and new, so it was hard to tell if anything was different or wrong.

"Where are you?" he called into the darkness, and was rewarded by another howl from nearby.

Neil's dad — who knew just about everything

there was to know about dogs — had once told him that howling was a dog's cry of loneliness. It was a pack instinct to beckon the other dogs to join him.

"What's wrong?" Neil said encouragingly, hoping the creature could hear him. "Are you lonely? Where are you?"

Just then the moon peeked out from behind the cloud and lit up the road.

Neil gasped.

Sitting in the center of the road ahead was a dog. Neil stood rooted to the spot.

It was a wirehaired dachshund and as his fur caught the moonlight he seemed to shimmer, looking almost spooky in the silvery night.

"There you are!" Neil said, looking carefully at the lonely dog. He tried to speak in a normal tone to conceal his unease. "What's wrong with you?"

The dog looked back at Neil. He was a fine little dachshund, stocky and solid with a thick wiry coat. But his deep-brown eyes seemed very sad. He lifted his head and howled again, his cry echoing in the darkness.

"Have you hurt yourself, boy? Got a thorn in your paw?" Neil asked, taking a slow step toward the dog so that he wouldn't startle it. "Let's see if I can help."

But the dog took off, running quickly on his short legs without a trace of a limp or injury.

"So it's not a thorn. Come back! I can't help you if you run away."

The dog stopped and looked back at Neil, then ran on.

Neil knew dogs well enough to recognize the signs. This dog wanted Neil to follow him. So he did.

They walked briskly until the dog came to the fork in the road. Without pausing, it took the path that led away from the village and toward the cliff.

"This is the cliff path," Neil muttered. He hesitated. "What do you want here that's so urgent in the middle of the night?"

The dog looked back at Neil, sat down, and howled

again. The noise was awful. Neil gave in and reluctantly walked down the cliff path.

"I hope it's worth it when we get there. Wherever you're taking me, it's obviously very important to *you*," he mumbled.

It was bitter cold on the cliff. Far below him, Neil could hear the waves breaking on the rocks and he smelled the salt spray in the air. As he made his way slowly along the muddy pathway, he realized that there was no barrier between him and the sea. If he slipped, he thought, he could plunge right over and be swept away to sea, never to be seen again!

Telling himself not to let his imagination run away with him, Neil went on, following the dog. Sometimes the dachshund seemed closer, but never quite close enough to touch. He wasn't wearing a collar, so there was no chance of grabbing him by that.

Along the cliff path, the grass and bushes were damp with dew. As he brushed against them the dog's coat seemed to pick up drops of water, making him glimmer and shine even more in the moonlight. Neil had the strangest feeling that if he reached out to touch the dog, he would just slip through his fingers, shadowy and unreal.

Suddenly, Neil found that the path ahead was hidden in a dense patch of sea mist. He turned around and could see nothing behind either. It was like standing in a cloud. He stopped, seriously scared. One false move . . .

The dog howled again.

"You'll have to wait until this mist has blown past," Neil called. "I'm not taking another step until it does."

And then, as quickly as it had arrived, the mist blew on, leaving the path clear again.

Completely clear. The dog had vanished.

"Hey!" Neil said, looking all around. "Where are you?"

This time, there was no answering howl.

The path ahead was fairly straight, with no bushes large enough for a dog to hide behind. There was no sign of him at all. It was as if the mist had just picked him up and spirited him away, Neil thought.

"So where have you gone?" Neil asked into the emptiness. "You must be *somewhere*."

Neil stood for a moment, reasoning with himself. A dog like the dachshund — an active, noisy dog — wouldn't just fall over the cliff without a single yelp. Besides, he was probably a local dog who walked on the cliffs every day and knew them like the back of his paw.

Neil turned and began to retrace his footsteps, trying to avoid the occasional puddles. He listened for the dog's howl, but all he could hear was the sea pounding on the rocks below. Hurrying off the cliff path, he started up the road that led back to the cottage, wondering what could have happened to the dog. He didn't want to give up on him but he was feeling the chill and the tips of his fingers and toes were getting numb.

Neil let himself back into the cottage quietly and crept upstairs. He didn't remember to take off his sneakers until it was too late; when he looked at the floor behind him he'd left muddy footprints all across the bedroom carpet.

Neil grimaced but quickly undressed and climbed back into bed anyway, pulling the covers tightly around him. He'd kept his sweatshirt on for extra warmth.

What a strange thing, he thought as he settled in again: a dog who'd howled the place down until he'd gone out to help him — and then disappeared into thin air.

And there was another strange thing, Neil thought. Just before he dropped off to sleep, he realized what it was. When he'd retraced his steps along the muddy path, he'd seen his footprints — but he hadn't seen any paw marks.

CHAPTER TWO

Neil was awakened by Emily throwing a pillow onto his bed.

"Wake up, lazy!" she said. "It's eight-thirty and we're on vacation!"

Neil groaned. He didn't usually sleep late. But then he didn't usually go around chasing dogs in the middle of the night, either.

"We've got things to do!" Emily called over. "I want to explore."

As the pale autumn sun crept across Neil's bed he stretched and yawned, looking forward to the week ahead. Compton was OK, but it was miles from the sea. There would be the cliffs and shore to explore, and maybe even a few caves and shipwrecks.

"I had a really weird dream about you last night,"

Emily said. "I dreamed that you got up in the middle of the night and went out looking for a dog. I dreamed that —"

Neil sat up suddenly. "I did," he interrupted. "I walked along the cliff path!" He pointed to his muddy sneakers and dirt-spattered jeans. "Look! That proves it."

"What happened?" Emily asked, sitting up and looking at him expectantly. "*Was* there a dog? Did you find it?"

Neil shrugged. "Yes . . . I don't know. It was a dachshund but I never managed to get hold of him. He just kept howling and running away. I followed him but I never seemed to reach where he wanted to go."

"Then what happened?"

"He just disappeared into thin air. Or mist, actually," he said thoughtfully.

Emily's eyes gleamed. "It sounds very exciting," she said. "I like the idea of a mysterious dog who disappears into the mist!"

"Maybe we can go out today with Sam and investigate," said Neil.

Emily was out of bed in a flash. "I'm taking my shower right now!"

"Hey, Em!" Neil said, as she disappeared around the door with her towel. "Don't say anything to Mom and Dad about me going out, will you?"

"Of course not!" Emily said. "I want to go out with

you next time — and if I tell them, there won't *be* a next time!"

"Did you sleep all right?" Carole Parker asked Neil and Emily as she put a plate of toast on the kitchen table.

"Fine, thanks," Neil said immediately.

"I slept like a dog!" little Sarah put in, removing the end of one of her pigtails from her mouth and inserting a piece of toast instead.

Beside her, Bob Parker laughed. He was a big, heavyset man with dark hair and a scruffy new beard. "I think that's meant to be 'like a *log*' — but in our case, maybe 'dog' is better."

"The sea air will do wonders for all of us," said Carole.

"That, and the wonderful quiet here," Bob added. "When I woke up this morning I had a strange feeling that something was missing but I couldn't think what it was. Then I realized what was so odd — it was the silence. There was no dawn chorus of barks!"

"You didn't hear a dog howling, then?" asked Emily.

Bob shook his head and frowned. "Dog? What time was that?" He was like Neil — any mention of a dog in trouble and he was all ears.

Neil kicked Emily under the table and gave her a meaningful glance.

"Oh, I don't know," Emily said. "Midnight, maybe. I probably imagined it."

Bob took his dish to the sink. "I'm going to make a few phone calls."

"Oh?" Carole said, smiling. "One guess where to?"

"King Street Kennels!" said Sarah.

Everyone laughed. Bob absolutely loved his dogs, so it was fairly amazing that he'd agreed to leave them in the first place. Having done so, though, he fully intended to stay in touch!

Half an hour later, Neil and Emily closed the kitchen door behind them before setting off to retrace Neil's movements during the night.

As they stood with Sam at the end of the over-grown garden of Summerbreeze, Neil thought about what his mom would say if she knew he'd already been on the cliff in the middle of the night.

"We shouldn't tire Sam too much," warned Neil, as he bent down to scratch Sam's furry white coat. "He needs his regular walks, of course — but no marathons."

Emily zipped up her jacket. "We won't go too far, then. Sam has to be our top priority."

They walked down the road toward the village, taking the cliff path at the fork in the road as Neil had done.

A couple of minutes later, Neil and Emily stopped outside the garden gate of a small, thatched cottage set back from the road. Neil hadn't noticed it the night before. In the garden, a tall woman with gray hair in braids was pruning roses. Beside the door, in a basket, was a small, fat dog.

"Oh, look!" Emily said, feeling slightly disap-pointed that their search might be over so quickly. "Is that your nighttime howler?"

Neil peered more closely. "No, that's a Yorkshire terrier. I definitely saw a wirehaired dachshund. But we can ask the woman if she knows of any other dogs around here."

At the sight of another dog, Sam poked his nose through the gate and barked, anxious to make friends. The Yorkie lifted his head, looked at Sam disdainfully, and closed its eyes again to go back to sleep. A frilly, pink bow was perched on its head.

"Excuse me," Neil said to the woman. "Could you tell us if anyone nearby owns a dachshund?"

The woman wore an assortment of multicolored scarves and sweaters over her dress, topped off with a bright purple shawl. Emily thought that she looked like a walking yard sale.

The woman turned and, at the sight of Neil, looked startled.

"Sorry," Neil said. "Did we make you jump? We just wondered . . ."

"It's not that," said the woman, frowning deeply. "You look a lot like . . ." She wiped her hands on her long, flowery dress.

Neil felt a bit embarrassed at the way the woman was looking at him. "I'm Neil Parker and this is my sister Emily. We're staying up at Summerbreeze," he explained.

"I see," said the woman suspiciously. "So you haven't been here before, then?"

Emily shook her head. "Never. Our dad works with the son of Mr. Turner, who owns the cottage — he's the vet where we live."

The woman continued to stare at Neil in an unfriendly way.

"We were just wondering if there were any other dogs around here," Emily added chattily.

"I heard a dog howling in the night, you see," explained Neil. "I followed it along this path."

"Well, it certainly wasn't my Prunella Pink," the woman said, indicating the dog in the basket.

Neil shook his head. "No, it was a dachshund."

The woman pursed her lips. "There aren't any dachshunds around here."

Neil and Emily exchanged glances. Why was the woman acting so strangely toward them?

"Well, OK," Neil said. He patted his leg for Sam to come along. "Thanks anyway. See you later."

"Good-bye!" Emily added with a polite smile.

They went on, past the cottage and toward the cliff.

"She was a funny one," Emily said, when they got out of earshot. "She was really strange to you."

Neil nodded. "Yeah. Even though she has a dog, I got the idea she doesn't really like them."

"She certainly doesn't like dachshunds!" Emily said.

"You're so right. She got all weird when I mentioned them."

"She's strange, if you ask me," Emily said, giggling. "Come on, let's keep looking."

Walking on, they reached one of the cliff's observation points.

"Wow!" Emily said, looking out to the horizon and taking in gulps of salty air. "Nothing but water for miles and miles. All I can see are seagulls and sea!"

Neil checked that Sam was safely by his side, then peered over the cliff edge. "Don't look down!" he said to Emily.

Emily did, of course. "Look at those big rocks! Can you imagine falling on them?"

"I'd rather not," replied Neil.

Half-buried on the sandy shore beside a line of black boulders was the rusting hull of an old cargo boat.

Emily nodded toward it excitedly. "Do you think there'll be anything still on board?"

Neil screwed up his nose. "Nah! There's hardly anything left of it."

Emily looked farther along the cliff path where they were standing. "So how far along here do you think you came last night?"

Neil examined the ground and continued to walk on. "Right up to where the cliff juts out," he said. "I think it's called Zennor Point."

Suddenly, he caught a movement on the path ahead. It was the dachshund. "There!" he said, pointing excitedly. "*There's* the dog!"

"I see him!" cried Emily.

The dachshund was sitting patiently ahead of them. His thick coat shone softly in the sunlight.

"Come on!" said Neil. He called Sam to heel. "Stay close, Sam. I don't want to have to do any cliff rescues."

Neil, Sam, and Emily started off in single file on

the narrow path, but as they got closer to the dachshund he trotted away.

Neil and Emily instinctively followed the animal, which turned around every so often to make sure that they were still there.

"What do you think he wants?" Emily asked quietly.

Neil shrugged. "He's got something for us, I expect. Something he wants us to see."

"Sam doesn't seem that interested in him, does he?" Emily said. Sam was trotting alongside them and wasn't taking the keen interest he normally took in other dogs.

Neil looked down at his dog. "I'm not surprised. There are too many other new things around here for him to look at — the waves crashing and the grasses waving and the seagulls calling. I bet Sam can't take everything in at once."

When Neil looked up again at the path, he stopped dead. "Hey! Where'd the dachshund go?"

Emily's attention had been on Sam, too. She looked around. "He's disappeared."

Neil ruffled his spiky hair. "This is just like what happened last night," said Neil, baffled.

"Let's keep walking and see if there's any trace of him."

Eventually the path ended as the three of them reached Zennor Point, the farthermost tip of the cliffs on the headland. They stood and stared at them, marveling at the vast expanse of ocean that seemed to surround them on all sides.

"Where did the dog go, Sam?" Neil asked.

Sam just sat and looked up at him, panting slightly.

"He couldn't have run ahead of us," Emily said, bending over, slightly out of breath. "There's nowhere to go."

"He couldn't have doubled back."

"And he definitely couldn't have gone down —" Emily began, and then broke off with a little shriek. "He *did* go down! Look!" She pointed down past the craggy cliff edge. "There he is on that strip of sand!"

She and Neil stared at the dog on the shoreline far beneath them. "How could he have gotten down there so quickly?" Neil asked in amazement. "It's too steep. There's no real path."

The dog looked up at them and began to howl.

"That's just what he was doing last night," Neil said. "That's what got me out of bed."

"Maybe there *is* a way down," Emily said, straining to see over the cliff without going too close to the edge.

Neil dropped onto his hands and knees and went forward as far as he dared. "Nope!" he said, peering down. "No path that I can see — it's just a sheer drop."

"So how did he get there? I don't like it," Emily

said, shivering. "I just read a book about a mad dog who lured people to their deaths!"

"Don't be ridiculous!" Neil scoffed. "This isn't a mad dog. It's just a lonely dachshund who wants to be friends."

"I hope you're right!" said Emily. "Because things are starting to get just a teeny bit weird around here."

CHAPTER THREE

"**T**he strange woman's house is around the next bend," Emily said to Neil as they walked away from Zennor Point. They'd searched the cliffs but found nothing. Either the dog could fly, or he knew a hidden path. Whichever, there was nothing Neil and Emily could do to follow him so they'd decided to make their way to the village instead.

"I hope the other local people are friendlier than her," Neil replied. "Even her dog didn't want to make friends! She wouldn't even *look* at Sam — she was too lazy even to lift her head!"

Emily laughed. "Prunella Pink!" she said in a silly voice. "Who names their dog Prunella Pink?"

"It's a shame," Neil said, smiling, too. "Yorkies are normally excellent little dogs."

"She hasn't taken care of hers, though," Emily said. "It's awful!"

"Pity," Neil said. "If we lived down here, we could offer to take old Prunes for walks. We'd soon get her into shape."

Emily stopped short. "Well, why don't we anyway? We'll be walking Sam every day. We could offer to take Miss Pink along with us."

Neil made a face. "It's a good idea — but she'd never let us."

"Come on. It's worth a try," said Emily, pressing on.

Neil shrugged and whistled for Sam. "OK."

In a few minutes, they were outside the woman's garden gate. She was standing pruning her roses on the path, looking as eccentric as she had earlier.

"Excuse me," Emily said politely. "We were wondering if you'd like us to exercise . . . er . . . your dog . . . er . . . Prunella Pink for you."

The woman put down her clippers. She stared at them without moving.

"We'll be walking our dog every day, you see," Neil added, pointing at Sam, "and we'd love to have another dog along with us."

"Prunella Pink doesn't like exercise," the woman said eventually.

Neil resisted the temptation to disagree with her. "Dogs are *much* healthier and live longer if they are exercised regularly, you know."

The woman looked at Neil hard. "And you're some sort of dog expert are you, young man?"

"Our parents run a boarding kennel," Neil said matter-of-factly.

"And our dad runs obedience classes for dogs as well," added Emily.

"We've also got a dog rescue center. Sam here was abandoned once and I've brought him up since he was a puppy. We love dogs — all kinds of dogs."

Sam barked a greeting as if on cue.

"Our friends at home call us the Puppy Patrol!" Emily said.

The woman hesitated. Her expression seemed to soften a little. "And you say you've never been to this village before?" she asked, looking at Neil again. "Are you sure?"

Neil nodded. "We've never been to Cornwall before."

"So you're not a Penrose?"

Neil looked bewildered. "A Penrose? What's that?"

The woman's face hardened again and she flicked her head toward a hill, at the top of which, through tall dark trees, was a gaunt gray house. "That's the Penrose house!" she cried. "And a bad bunch they are, too!"

There was a long silence. Neither Emily nor Neil knew what to say. Even Sam stared up at the woman, puzzled.

"So is it OK if we take Prunella for a quick walk

down to the village?" Emily asked the woman. She nudged Neil to move.

The woman hesitated. "Well, you shouldn't tire her out if you do. And she must be back at lunchtime for her chocolate milk and her cookies. And it's chilly, so she must wear her waterproof jacket . . ."

Fifteen minutes later, after numerous preparations for the outing by the Yorkie's doting owner, Neil and Emily were walking toward the village again. Prunella, wearing a sparkly collar and matching waterproof jacket, was trotting alongside them and seemed to be enjoying the outing.

"Oh, well," Emily said, "we've lost one dog and found another."

"I never thought Mrs. Strange would let us take Prunella," Neil said.

Emily rolled her eyes. "And what was all that other stuff about? This Penrose business?"

"Who knows?" Neil said. "But it makes you want to find out, doesn't it?" He looked at Prunella, then bent down to take off her jacket. "I don't mind the collar because you can't see it under her fur, but coats with sparkly pink sequins are out!"

Emily nodded, taking off the pink bow and ruffling the Yorkie's forehead so that it didn't look quite so smooth and groomed. "No wonder Sam won't have anything to do with her," she said. Sam was already forging ahead, picking up doggy scents, snuffling in the grass, and completely ignoring the fat Yorkshire terrier.

"If we can walk her every day we're here," Neil said, stuffing the dog's jacket in his pocket, "I'm sure it'll make quite a difference."

"We should ask Dad to have a word with Mrs. Strange about the dog's diet, too," Emily put in.

"Chocolate milk and cookies at lunchtime!" snorted Neil. "No wonder she's such a lump!"

By the time they reached the cobblestone road that led down to the harbor and the village, Prunella was visibly tired. She slumped down, panting, her fat little tummy bulging under her, and she refused to go any farther.

Emily looked at the dog and shook her head. "Prunes — I bet you haven't had a decent walk in years!"

"Well, we'd better not overdo it for today," said Neil, bending down to pick her up. "We'll carry you the rest of the way, but don't think you're getting away with it. You're walking back by yourself!"

Prunella settled herself snugly into Neil's arms. *This* was more like what she was used to!

They turned a corner and the shiny slate rooftops of the village came into view below them. There were a hundred or so cottages, mostly built of the local gray stone. A few small shops dotted the landscape — along with two ancient restaurants and a tiny, modern-looking church. The long, U-shaped harbor framed the scene very nicely and the whole view seemed like a picture postcard.

"I wonder if anyone here in the village will know about our mystery dog?" Emily asked. The path wound its way down among the buildings on the outskirts of Tregarth.

"Well, someone must have seen him," said Neil.

Neil and Emily ended up near the harbor. The tide was out and there were a dozen or so fishing boats stuck in the mud, waiting for the water to return.

Sam sniffed the salty air, caught the scent of dead fish, and didn't seem to want to investigate further.

"Let's hit the shops," Emily said. "I want to buy some rock candy as a present for Kate."

As they turned to go, Neil noticed a brass plaque set in a large flat stone in the harbor wall. "Wait! Look at this."

"What is it?"

"A piece of village history."

Neil read the inscription out loud.

In solemn and revered memory of the
following residents of Tregarth,
who lost their lives on Black Saturday:
Ivy Trevelyan
Barnaby Dawson
James Polzard
David Tredinnick
Robin Pearce

Emily noticed the date on the plaque. "That's almost exactly a hundred years ago," she said. "I wonder what happened."

"No idea," said Neil. "Very dramatic though. Black Saturday doesn't sound like much fun, does it?"

They began to walk toward the row of old-fashioned-looking shops, with Prunella still resting lazily in Neil's arms.

Neil suddenly gestured frantically across the narrow road with his head. "Do you see what's next door to the library?"

Emily looked. "Tregarth Village Museum," she read out from the flaking notice over the door.

"Just what we need," said Neil. "There's bound to be someone in there who'll be able to fill us in about Black Saturday."

Crossing over to the museum, Neil gave Prunella to Emily to carry, and put Sam on his leash. He pushed open the door of the small white building and went inside. Emily tentatively followed him with Sam in tow.

Inside, everything was dark and seemed very quiet.

"Do you think it's open?" Emily whispered.

"Hello!" Neil called out. "Is anyone there?"

Suddenly, a light flickered on above their heads and revealed a room full of glass cases, rusting anchors, and old wooden figureheads mounted on walls.

"Ahoy there!" A gruff voice came from somewhere at the back of the space.

"Hello!" Neil and Emily replied, blinking at the small man who came out of a side room and stood before them. He looked ancient, with leathery, weather-beaten skin and piercing blue eyes. His size, coupled with the red woolly hat he wore pulled well down over his head, made him look a bit like a garden gnome.

"Hello," Emily said nervously. "Are you open?"

"Do you mind if we look around?" said Neil.

"That's what we're here for!" the man replied jovially.

Neil stepped forward out of the shadowy doorway. "We wondered if you could —"

The man's reaction to Neil's face stopped him dead.

On catching sight of him, the museum curator dropped the book he'd been holding and sat down heavily on a chair nearby.

"By the bones of old Jeremiah!" he said, staring thunderstruck at Neil.

Neil's jaw dropped. *Now* what?

"Where did *you* come from, my lad?" asked the old man, pointing a trembling hand at Neil.

Neil swallowed hard. "From near Manchester," he said. "My name's Neil, and this is my sister Emily. We're on vacation here with our mom and dad."

"As I live and breathe!" said the curator. "Nicholas Penrose!"

Neil was too flabbergasted to reply, but Emily spoke up quickly. "I'm sorry, but we don't know who Nicholas Penrose is. We've got nothing to do with him. And we've never ever been here before," she added for good measure.

"We're only here for a week," said Neil, desperately trying to explain.

The curator shook his head. "Incredible!"

Neil and Emily both began to think the old man was senile. He wasn't making any sense. Then he turned and beckoned them through to another murkily lit room that didn't seem to be part of the main museum at all.

The old man sighed as he flicked on a lamp just beside the door. Dust-covered clutter and old exhibits littered the floor and were piled up high on tables and broken chairs. The trembling curator pointed at a large oil painting on the wall in front of them. It was partially covered by a dirty white cloth that he dramatically whipped away, releasing a cloud of dust.

"Nicholas Penrose!" he announced. "See the likeness!"

Neil and Emily stared incredulously at the painting of a boy with a dog.

"It's you!" Emily cried. "He's just like you, Neil!"

The boy, in spite of his old-fashioned clothes, was almost Neil's twin. Underneath the painting was a small steel sign that said, NICHOLAS PENROSE•LEST WE FORGET, with a date.

"He's even got your hair sticking up in front!" Emily gasped.

"But . . . but it's *not* me, is it?" Neil said shakily. "How could it be?"

"And the dog, Neil! Look at the dog!" Emily whispered. "It's just like our mystery dog, isn't it?"

With another thump of shock, Neil saw that the dog with Nicholas Penrose was a wirehaired dachshund. He shook his head in bewilderment. Strange

things were happening in Tregarth — things that he
didn't like very much. "This was painted *years* ago.
Almost a hundred years ago, in fact," he said, looking
at the date under the inscription.

The curator let out an hysterical laugh. "Nicholas
Penrose reborn! What a thought!" He looked at Neil.
"Tell me, son, have other people in this village been
looking at you strangely?"

Neil shrugged. "We only arrived here last night."

"Prune's owner was a bit funny with you, Neil —
and she mentioned the name Penrose," Emily said.

NICHOLAS PENROSE
"LEST WE FORGET"
~1899~

"A couple of funny things *have* happened," Neil admitted to the man. "We came in here hoping to find an explanation."

"Ah, well, you might find some answers," he replied cautiously. "But you might not like them."

"So who *is* Nicholas Penrose?" asked Neil slowly.

The curator, with a bony finger, beckoned them back toward the side office from which he'd emerged earlier. "We can talk in here."

Emily and Neil exchanged glances. Sam, feeling there was some threat to his master, gave a low growl.

"Do you think we ought to run for it?" Emily whispered to Neil as the man left the room.

Neil shook his head and pulled his gaze away from the oil painting. "We haven't done anything wrong. Come on, let's find out what this is all about. . . ."

CHAPTER FOUR

The old man pointed to two stools in the cramped office, indicating where Neil and Emily should sit. They did so, Neil depositing a surprised Prunella on the hard floor. Sam stood guard over her.

For a while the old man didn't say anything; he just stared at Neil and kept clicking his teeth and shaking his head.

After a moment or two of this, Neil repeated his question. "Who is — or was — Nicholas Penrose?"

"And what did he do that was so terrible?" Emily added.

The curator drew in a deep breath. "Nicholas Penrose was a Tregarth boy. He disappeared like a shameful coward when he was eleven, almost a hundred years ago."

Neil let out a cry of surprise. "So he must have been born exactly a hundred years before me. Because I'm eleven *now*!"

"Oh, wow!" Emily cried.

The curator nodded. "What goes around, comes around," he murmured knowingly.

Neil and Emily looked at each other — neither had the slightest idea what the old man meant. After a moment, Neil coughed loudly to encourage the man to continue.

"The Penroses were a fine, noble line," the man began again, "until Nicholas ruined their reputation."

"Do any of them still live here?" Emily asked. "We've seen the Penrose house on the cliff."

"Victor Penrose still lives in the house," the curator answered. "But he's seen the best years of his life grow dim. He'd be the nephew of Nicholas Penrose."

"What happened to him?" Emily asked, feeling that she would burst if she didn't find out soon.

"All in good time," the old man replied. He took another deep breath. "Young Nicholas Penrose had the best of everything: a good education, fine clothes, a private tutor, and a stable of horses. But it wasn't enough for him. When he was eleven years old he ran off and went bad."

"What do you mean?" Neil asked.

"He argued with his father and vowed to make his own way in the world — then he left and fell in with a band of pirates."

"Wow!" Neil said, thinking that he couldn't imagine anything more exciting than that.

"It wasn't as you think, son," said the curator. "They weren't just jolly sailors making merry and stealing apples. Although that's what Nicholas Penrose may have thought at first. Oh, no, they were an evil, murderous bunch who didn't have a decent bone among them. And in the end, Nicholas Penrose turned as evil as the rest of them."

"But . . . but he was only eleven!" Emily said. "Didn't his mom and dad try to get him back?"

"They did," said the curator, "but he wouldn't have anything to do with them. When he left the house he didn't take anything — except his dog."

Neil felt prickles run down his spine. "A wire-haired dachshund . . ." he murmured.

"Like in the painting. We've seen a dachshund up on the cliffs!" Emily said in an awestruck whisper.

The man didn't seem to hear her. "Jeremiah Bones, the dog was named," he went on. "Nicholas Penrose had him since he was a puppy and they were inseparable."

"Jeremiah Bones," Neil echoed. So was the dog that he'd seen a descendant of the original dog? Neil instinctively held Sam tight to his side and gently stroked the collie's muzzle resting on his knee.

"Did Nicholas and the dog live with the pirates?" Emily asked.

The old man nodded. "For several months they lived on board the pirate ship, the *Dark Lady,* which was moored in a little creek concealed between two points in the cliff face. At night the ruffians would go out and rob passing boats, like highwaymen of the seas. And sometimes they would lure ships onto the rocks, and then plunder them for their treasure. The authorities had lost control and didn't seem to be able to stop them. But then one Saturday in October, nearly a hundred years ago —"

"Was that Black Saturday?" Neil interrupted.

"It was," the old man said, "and the darkest night in this village's history! On Black Saturday, not content with stealing from ships at sea, the pirates turned toward the village for their thieving. There was talk that their hideaway had finally been discovered and that the police were coming. On that night the pirates came into the village and ran wild, looting and robbing wherever they could."

The old man gathered a deep breath, his eyes glinting. "They smashed windows and set fire to thatch, taking everything they could carry, harming old and young, men and women alike. Five people died that night, including my grandfather, David Tredinnick, who was caught in the cross fire between those monsters and the police. My father was a boy of ten at the time, and still had nightmares till the day he died, thirty years ago."

Neil and Emily looked at each other in horror.

"We saw that name on the memorial," Emily said in a whisper.

The old man continued. "They not only killed, but they took gold and silver from the church and then burned it to the ground."

"And was . . . was Nicholas Penrose part of all this?" Neil asked shakily.

"Of course he was! And ten times worse than the pirates, for he'd turned against his own. It was he who must have told the murderous band where the best pickings were to be found. They knew exactly where to go."

"So what happened to him in the end?" Emily asked.

The old man paused. "He was never seen again after Black Saturday. Nor were the pirates. They sailed the *Dark Lady* away to another port. Some said they went abroad. Nobody really cared. Our village was left to pick up the pieces."

"And did the dog — did Jeremiah sail away with them, too?" Neil asked.

The curator shook his head. "Jeremiah stayed," he said, "and for years afterward, he sat on the cliff and howled for his master to come home. But of course he never did."

Neil scratched his head, bewildered. "I can't believe that Nicholas didn't take his dog with him. You said they were inseparable."

"They were."

"Then why . . . ?"

"Seems the boy had lost the decency even for that," said the curator. "He left his dog to howl for him for years and years. Jeremiah Bones lived on the cliffs, looking out for his master, until he died of old age and was taken back to Penrose Manor to be buried. It was the only place that would have him."

Emily turned to Neil wide eyed. "But the dog we saw . . . you don't think that . . ."

Neil shrugged, bewildered, then spoke up. "Does anyone around here own a dachshund?" he asked.

"Not that I know of. Dachshunds still aren't very popular dogs in this village."

"Still?" Emily cried. "I know it was awful but it all happened years ago. A *hundred* years ago!"

"But we grandchildren of the victims are still here," said the old man. He got up slowly from behind his desk and hobbled toward the door with his head hung low. "Stories are passed on through the generations. My own father knew Nicholas Penrose as a boy and used to spit on the ground whenever his name was mentioned." He looked at Neil briefly and his eyes glinted. Then he left the room saying, "You should just watch yourself around here, son . . ."

"I can't get over it," Neil said as they walked up the hill out of the village. "It's just such a coincidence — how Nicholas Penrose looks so much like me, and was born exactly a hundred years before me."

Emily shook her head. "It's bizarre." She stopped and tugged on Prunella's leash. The round little Yorkie was lying stretched out on the grass at the side of the path. "She's had enough walking again. We're going to have to carry her the rest of the way."

"That's OK," Neil said. "She's done pretty well today, considering she's carrying twice as much weight on those legs as she's supposed to." He went back to pick up the little dog, looking around as he did so. "I was hoping we might see our dachshund on the way home."

"Jeremiah Bones?" said Emily.

"Jeremiah's descendant, perhaps," said Neil. He scrunched up his face. "Em," he said slowly. "I'm not sure about Nicholas Penrose."

"What do you mean?"

"I'm not sure he was as terrible as they're trying to make out."

"Of course he was! He led the pirates to the village, didn't he?"

"How do you know that for sure?"

Emily shrugged. "History. Because everyone in the village says so."

"I think . . . well, I bet there's more to it than meets the eye."

"You're just saying that because he looks like you and because you don't want to have a connection with someone so wicked!"

"It's not just that," Neil said slowly. "I think that

anyone who'd had a dog as their best friend since it was a puppy . . ."

". . . couldn't be all bad?" Emily offered.

"Not just that . . . he couldn't go off and leave him," Neil said. He looked at Sam, who was rolling in the long grass beside Prunella. Neil called the dog over and rubbed his head.

"There's no way that I could ever leave Sam. Anywhere. For any reason. So I've just got a feeling about it — a feeling that there's something more to learn. And maybe this dog we've seen is trying to help us find out what it is."

Emily laughed. "Don't be ridiculous! Nicholas Penrose must be guilty . . . But I suppose I'm open to being persuaded otherwise!"

"Great!" said Neil. "It can be our vacation project: to solve the mystery of what *really* happened to Nicholas Penrose!"

"And find out about the vanishing dachshund, too," added Emily.

As Prunella's cottage came into view Neil stopped abruptly. "Hang on!" he said, feeling inside his pocket. "Prune's coat!"

"And the bow!" Emily said.

They put the jeweled jacket on the dog, retied the bow in her hair, and generally cleaned her up before they knocked on the door. Sam, covered in bits of grass and dusty from rolling around on the road, looked curiously at all the fuss they were making.

Prunella's fond owner greeted her dog as if she'd been away for a month.

"Hot choccy for my baby!" They heard her cooing as she took the little dog inside. "Yummy cookies!"

Neil and Emily groaned. They said a quick, polite good-bye and, laughing, ran back down the road toward Summerbreeze.

Neil held the phone to his ear and let out a shout. "I heard him!" he said. "I heard Jake bark."

His dad chuckled. "I don't know how I let myself get talked into this," he said. Neil had persuaded him to call Old Mill Farm — where Sam and Delilah's puppy, Jake, was — so that Neil could check on his progress.

"It's a good thing Sarah's in bed," Carole Parker said to Emily, "or she'd want to call home to listen to her hamster!"

"When do you think I can take Jake, Dad?" Neil asked when he'd put the phone down.

"When he's ten weeks old, I think," Bob said. "Just before Christmas."

"He's making good progress apparently," Neil went on. "Biggest in the litter, Jane Hammond says!" He rubbed his head into Sam's fur. "Hear that, Sam?"

Bob nodded. "You'll see some changes in the pup by the time we get back."

"I wonder if he'll look like Sam when he's fully grown," Neil mused, staring at Sam. "I wonder if Sam will know Jake is his son?"

"Ah, that's something we'll never know," said Bob. He put down the newspaper he was reading. "So where does this fat little Yorkie live?"

"In the cottage by the fork in the road," Neil said.

"The one with the pretty garden," his mom added.

"Dad, we'd like you to come along with us there sometime," Emily said, "and see if you can chat with Mrs. Strange about Prunes's diet."

"I don't think you should call her Mrs. Strange,"

Carole said with mock sternness, "even if she *is*. What's her real name?"

Emily frowned. "Not sure. But there was a plaque on the gate saying *Pendragon.*"

Carole Parker nodded. "Anyway, your dad can't interfere with the care of other people's dogs, you know. Not without being asked."

"You don't have to interfere, Dad," Neil said, "just drop a few hints to Mrs. . . . Pendragon about 'hot choccy' not helping a dog's teeth — or something."

"If the opportunity presents itself, I'll see what I can do," Bob promised.

Emily got up and stretched. "I'm going to bed," she said. "We've got a busy day tomorrow."

"Another one of your wild-goose chases, if you ask me," said Bob.

"More investigations?" Carole asked with a smile. Neil and Emily had already told their parents everything about Nicholas Penrose, Jeremiah Bones, and Black Saturday.

Emily nodded enthusiastically. "We thought we might go to the library and see if they've got any local records or newspapers from that time that covered the event."

"*And* we've got to see if we can find out who owns the mysterious disappearing dachshund!" added Neil.

"If anyone does," said Emily. "It might be a *ghost* dog . . ."

"Don't be silly," said Bob dismissively. "You two

should know better than to talk about ghosts and such."

Emily made a loud ghostly moaning noise that Sam tried to join in with.

Neil hid his face with his arm and moaned in embarrassment.

CHAPTER FIVE

*O*n the cliff edge, a thick mist swirled and it was difficult for Neil to make out the blurred, shadowy figure standing in front of him.

The figure took a step forward and Neil saw that it was Nicholas Penrose as he appeared in the museum portrait. "You've got to help me," he pleaded, holding out his hand.

Neil felt a prickle of fright run down his back. "I don't know if I can. I don't know how."

"But you're the one I've been waiting for. You're the one who can clear my name."

"It's got nothing to do with me!" Neil said.

"You can help my surviving family! I must rest easy in my grave. Until our name is cleared there can be no peace for me — or for Jeremiah."

"What am I supposed to do?" Neil asked. *"We're only here for a week. I can't . . ."*

"You must follow my good dog. Follow where he leads!" Nicholas cried, and the shadowy figure began to fade.

"Hang on!" Neil said. *"What do you mean by follow your dog? Don't go yet. You've got to tell me what to do . . ."*

But the figure blurred and dissolved into the mist until it finally vanished altogether.

"Come back!" Neil said.

"Neil!" Emily's voice came into her brother's dream and woke him. "Stop muttering to yourself. You woke me up and it's much too early."

Neil turned over on his back and looked up at the ceiling, where the first thin rays of sun were coming into the room. *Only a dream,* he thought. But Nicholas had seemed so real, and had spoken so intently. "I was dreaming about Nicholas Penrose," he said to his sister. "He said we've got to help him. Follow his dog."

"We'll follow his dog later," Emily said sleepily. "It's only seven o'clock and we're on vacation. Go back to sleep!"

But Neil couldn't. He lay in bed and went over everything Nicholas had said, wondering what it all meant, wondering what *he* could possibly do to help. He didn't think he believed in ghosts. Or in ghost dogs. But suddenly his dream had made it all so real and he was more determined than ever to find out the truth.

After breakfast, Neil's mom handed him a list. "I want you and Emily to go into the village for me. There's a bakery there where they bake their own breads and pastries fresh every day."

Bob Parker laughed. "We'll go home as fat as pigs," he said. Then he eyed the phone and wondered if it was too early to call King Street Kennels.

"You aren't in a hurry for this stuff, are you, Mom?" Neil asked, as he and Emily got themselves ready to go out. "Because Emily and I have other things to do while we're there."

"Just as long as they don't sell out of those pastries!" his mother replied.

On the way to the village, Neil and Emily stopped to pick up Prunella.

"She *did* sleep well last night," said Mrs. Pendragon — who'd added a sparkly red shawl to her layers of scarves and sweaters. "I think her walkies did her good!"

"Well, we've come to see if she'd like another . . . walkies," Neil said, nudging Emily.

Prunella was brought out, cooed over, brushed, petted, and had a fresh bow tied in her hair. Mrs. Pendragon finally stood back and seemed satisfied

that Prunella Pink was ready for her walk. "And remember —"

"We know," Emily said, "get her back for her hot
choccy and cookies!"

"Precisely," said Mrs. Pendragon.

This time, Prunella almost made it to the cobblestone path into the village before she came to a full
stop. As Emily picked her up to carry her the rest of
the way, Sam looked at her and gave a little bark as
if to say he was quite disgusted.

"She'd never make a sheepdog, would she, Sam?"
Neil said, patting his dog's back. "But she's done a
little better today. She's improving."

"That's because she's following the Puppy Patrol
plan!" Emily said.

Neil grinned and ruffled the Yorkie's forehead.

Leaving Emily with the dogs outside the bakery,
Neil went inside to buy his mother's pastries and a
large crusty loaf of bread. When he came out with
several paper bags, Sam sniffed at them so enthusiastically that a bag got torn and Neil had to go back
inside for a plastic one.

Order restored, carrying Prunella and keeping
Sam on a close leash, they went to the library.

"We're not sure exactly what we want," Neil said
to the librarian, and then hesitated because of the
surprised and openly curious expression of the young
woman behind the counter.

"Excuse me," she said, "I know you're not a local but your face is very familiar. Where have I seen you before?"

Neil sighed. This sort of reaction to his appearance was getting a bit embarrassing.

"This is my brother Neil," Emily said, coming to his rescue, "and we know he just happens to look like Nicholas Penrose."

"That's it!" the librarian said.

"We're not related to the Penroses or anything," Emily said.

"Honestly we're not," Neil added, thinking that at

this rate he was going to have to put on a fake nose and glasses whenever he went out. "We're on vacation here," he explained, "but . . . well, because of this likeness I have to Nicholas Penrose, I'm interested in finding out more about him. Things about Black Saturday and so on. Can you help?"

"We thought you might have some old newspapers and other records from that time," said Emily.

The woman looked around hastily. "OK, you'd better come through to the reference section."

"Can the dogs come in, too?" Neil asked, looking at Sam below the level of the counter.

"Of course," the woman said. "I've got a spaniel myself, so I think that well-behaved dogs should be allowed to go anywhere they like. But don't tell my boss!"

She led Neil and Emily into the book-lined room, which was the reference section. "You've got an interesting project there," she said. "I'm not from Tregarth myself — I come from London — so I don't know much about this Black Saturday business. But I do know that the locals are still pretty touchy about it." She pointed to a stack of books underneath the window. "That's all local history there, and in that desk are old maps and some handwritten accounts of days gone by. Over there," she pointed, "are copies of the regional papers on microfilm. They go way back. Do you know how to use the equipment?"

Neil nodded.

"Then I'll leave you to it. Let me know if you want anything else." She bent down to pat Sam and Prunes, then looked at Neil curiously. "Funny you look so much like him, though . . ."

"Geez," Neil muttered after she'd left. "Ever felt like you're in a circus?"

"This is what it must be like to be famous," Emily said. "I'm glad it's you and not me!"

Neil settled Sam under the table, put Prunella on a chair where she promptly went to sleep, and got out the pad and pens he'd brought with him. "OK," he said, "first of all we want to know more about Black Saturday."

Emily nodded. "And then we've got to try and find out what's going on with that dog, as well." She chewed the end of a pen. "But maybe the dog's got nothing to do with anything. Maybe it's just a coincidence that he happens to be a dachshund — the same as Nicholas's."

"I think he *does* have something to do with it," Neil said, remembering the dream.

Emily giggled. "It all sounds pretty far-fetched."

"You're telling me it's far-fetched!" Neil said, absentmindedly breaking off a piece of pastry. "The whole thing is totally weird."

He went over to the box of microfilm. "Should I start with the newspapers and you start with the local history books?"

Emily nodded. "And we'll write down every new fact we discover."

Neil soon got the hang of the equipment and looked up anything under October from a hundred years before. He hit the jackpot right away.

"Hey!" he shouted to Emily. "Got it. Listen to this headline: *Villainous Pirates Attack Village.*"

Emily gasped, and left the books she was reading to go and look over Neil's shoulder. "*The Penrose family hang their heads in shame,*" she read out from the next edition.

She and Neil looked at each other.

"It's all here!" Neil said, eating another piece of pastry. "We've just got to piece it together."

"OK, so what have we got?" Neil said an hour later.

"Well, we've got the full story on Black Saturday now," Emily said. "We know where the houses were that were destroyed, and where the people lived who were killed by the pirates. There's also some background information on Nicholas's family."

Neil nodded. "We know that he had two younger brothers, and that the family tried to move away — leave the area altogether after Black Saturday — but no one would buy the house because they said it was cursed."

"We've also got these," Emily said, smoothing out

some photocopies of half a dozen of the newspaper
front pages.

ANGRY VILLAGERS STORM PENROSE HOUSE, the headlines on one said, and VILLAGE SEEKS REVENGE!

"It seems so unfair," Emily said slowly. "OK, what
Nicholas did was terrible, but he wasn't the one that
actually did the stealing and killing, was he?"

Neil shook his head. "According to these reports,
no one saw him with the pirates attacking the village that night."

"And anyway, it had nothing to do with his family.
Why did they get punished as well?"

"I suppose, with Nicholas and the pirates having
left, the villagers had no one else to turn their anger
on," Neil said. "I still can't understand how he could
leave his dog, though. How could he just sail away
and leave Jeremiah?" He bent down to ruffle Sam's
fur under the table.

"If he was as wicked and horrible as they say he
was . . ."

"But what if he wasn't?"

"OK, he might not have been," Emily said. "But
how are you going to find out the truth?"

"I don't know," Neil shrugged. "Let's drop Prunes
off up the road and think about it some more."

Emily sighed. "Wait! There's something else!" she
said suddenly. "Something very serious."

"What's that?" said Neil, alarmed.

"You've eaten two of those pastries we bought for lunch," Emily said. "What's Mom going to say?"

"There he is!" Neil exclaimed. He pointed wildly up the path.

"Who?" asked Emily, looking around. They'd stopped at the bakery for two more pastries, dropped off Prunella, and were now on their way back to Summerbreeze for lunch.

"Jeremiah Bones!" said Neil urgently. "He's sitting up there waiting for us!"

Emily looked back up the lane and nodded excitedly. "I can see him now!"

"Look, Sam!" Neil said. "Nice dog! Go and make friends!"

Sam looked at him, puzzled.

"Dog ahead!"

Sam looked up the road, then looked back at Neil.

"He either can't see him," said Emily, "or he's just not interested."

"Look, he's walking away," Neil murmured. "Let's not lose sight of him. We've got to follow him."

As before, the dachshund went along the cliff path.

Neil ran after the dog with Emily tugging Sam along behind on his leash. "Do we have to go so fast, though?" she puffed.

And then, when they were almost at Zennor Point, a thin mist rolled across the path and the dog seemed to vanish.

Neil stopped, exasperated. "He's gone again! I was watching him, Em. I didn't take my eyes off him. One minute he was trotting along the path, the next he'd disappeared."

Emily suddenly pointed below them and started laughing. "This is ridiculous," she said. "There he is again!"

"He can't be!" Neil said in amazement, looking over the edge. "He couldn't have gotten down there that quickly."

But he had. They stood and stared at the tiny figure of the dachshund on the strip of sand below.

"I know this is stupid, but I can think of only one explanation," Emily said. "There are two dogs. Twins. One runs into a hole, and at the same time the other one appears on the beach. Someone's playing tricks on us."

Neil shook his head. "There's another explanation, but I can't quite believe it," he said. "What if it *is* Jeremiah Bones — and he's a ghost? Ghosts can fly around and walk through walls and all that sort of stuff, so I bet a ghost could get down to the bottom of that cliff in no time at all."

They gazed down at the dog.

"He doesn't *look* like a ghost," Emily said.

"I know," Neil replied quietly. "And I don't even believe in ghosts."

"What do you think we ought to do, then?"

"Try and get down there ourselves," Neil said. He remembered his dream and added thoughtfully, "*We must follow his dog . . .*"

"We can't follow now," Emily said. "We've got to get back for lunch. Mom will be going crazy. It's already two o'clock."

Neil sighed and kicked the ground. The disappearing dachshund was driving him crazy with frustration. "Next time we go down there," he said angrily. "Next time, no matter what."

CHAPTER SIX

"**S**o this is the famous Prunella Pink, is it?" Bob Parker said, grinning. He picked up the little dog and seemed to weigh her in his hands. "Alert enough, but a bit heavy."

Bob looked into her eyes, and then her mouth. "Eyes are fine, but her teeth aren't very good, and neither are her gums."

"That's because she eats sweet cookies instead of hard dog biscuits!" Neil said.

The following morning Bob had decided, after making a few phone calls to King Street Kennels, that the whole family should take a brisk walk along the cliffs. Emily and Neil had gone ahead to get Prunella and then met their mom, dad, and Sarah on the cliff path.

"You do think it'll help, though — us walking her this week?" Neil asked.

Bob put Prunella down again and looked at her appraisingly. "Oh, it'll help. But only if her owner keeps it up — and only if she's exercised regularly from now on. *And* given some good hard chews for her teeth."

"Couldn't you tell her owner that?" Emily asked. "She'll listen to you. You're a dog expert."

Bob grinned. "I'm not a dog expert at the moment. I'm on vacation!"

Carole gave him a nudge. "You're always a dog expert!"

The family began to walk along the cliff path toward Zennor Point, with Sam in front, and Neil and Emily keeping an eagle eye open for their mystery dachshund.

When they reached the point, Bob Parker gestured back across the bay to where another cliff jutted out into the sea. "Around there, apparently, was Smugglers' Creek, where those pirates of yours had their hideaway."

"What?" Neil asked excitedly. "We read about that yesterday, but couldn't pinpoint where it was. Who told you about it?"

"Some old sea dog your mom and I met on our walk yesterday. He was full of ancient tales."

"A talking dog?" Sarah squealed. "We didn't meet a talking dog!"

"A sea dog," Carole explained, "is what people call an old sailor."

"He said that hidden away behind that jagged spur of rocks is an inlet of water," Bob went on. "Apparently the pirates used it as a hideaway; they steered their boats through the rocks and tied them up where they couldn't be seen from above. And right at the back, hidden in the cliff, was the cave they used as a hideout."

"They hid all their loot there, apparently," added Carole.

"Is it still there?" Neil asked. "I don't mean the loot — the cave."

His father shrugged. "Probably. The old boy hadn't been down there for years. But they get some pretty wild storms down here and the beach levels change all the time: boulders roll, the cliff face falls, and sand gets drawn up and shifted around. Often caves are closed up completely."

"Didn't he say something about it being accessible only during low tide?" Carole asked.

"Something like that," said Bob. "And even then only on foot." He was still looking at Prunella, more concerned with checking on her health than thinking about pirates' caves.

"I can see a rusty old boat on the sand," Sarah said, sounding disappointed, "but I can't see any pirates."

"There aren't any now," Carole said. "This was years and years ago."

"A hundred years," Neil said. He caught a movement down on the beach and grabbed Emily's arm. "Look!" he said, pointing. He called to his mom and dad, who'd begun to walk on. "Over there! Look — on the beach! There's the dog we've been talking about."

Bob and Carole shielded their eyes from the sun and looked down to the beach. "I can't see a dog," said Bob.

"Neither can I," said Carole.

"Can you see him, Squirt?" Neil asked his younger sister.

Sarah looked. "I *think* so," she said after a moment. "On the other side of the wreck — just by the black rock!"

The family and the two dogs stood staring at the rocks below.

"Why don't you go down there? The tide is out," suggested Bob.

"I don't think there's a path down," Emily said. "We've looked twice already."

"Nonsense," said Bob Parker matter-of-factly. "There's bound to be one here somewhere." He went toward the edge of the cliff and began parting some of the spindly bushes and long, tufty grasses. "Told you so. Hmm. It's very narrow, but it looks safe enough," he said slowly, letting his eyes move down the steep cliff path he had just discovered.

"That's weird," said Neil. "I couldn't see it yesterday."

"It was hidden pretty well, that's all," said Bob.

Neil turned inquisitively to Carole. "Should we all go down?"

"No thanks," his mom said immediately. "Even if we could get down, I don't like the idea of the climb back up!"

"I'll come with you, Neil," said Emily.

"Are you sure it's all right, Bob?" Carole asked.

"Yes, they'll be all right," Bob said. "As long as you're *very* careful. We'll walk along a little farther and come back for you."

"Great!" Emily and Neil said together.

Neil turned to Sam and ruffled his fur. "Stay here, boy. This hike might be a bit too tough for you. I won't be long! Hang on to Prunes for me, will you, Dad?"

Neil set off first, stepping carefully along the path that led down toward the beach. "How come we didn't see this yesterday?" he called to Emily behind him.

"I don't know," Emily said. "Maybe we didn't look carefully enough."

"I'm sure we did," Neil said, frowning.

"I can't talk," Emily said, eyes glued in concentration on the path. "I've got to think about where I'm putting my feet."

Slowly and carefully, they made their way down.

"Do you think the dachshund got down this way yesterday?" Emily asked as they finally reached the strip of sand at the bottom.

Neil shook his head. "That took twelve minutes," he said, looking at his watch. "He couldn't have gone down this way — even if he'd run as fast as his little hairy legs would carry him."

Emily waved up to Sarah on the path high above them. "So where's he gone now?" she asked.

"Over there!" Neil pointed across the rocks to where the dachshund was sitting, seemingly waiting for them. "Let's go!"

When they got to the rusting hull of the ship-wrecked boat, they stopped to have a closer look. Very little of it remained.

"It's not as exciting as it looks from above, is it?" Emily said, examining its rusty framework. Bits of rotten metal broke off in her hand.

There was a melancholy howl from farther along the sand and Emily and Neil looked over to the dachshund.

"We'd better go," Neil said. "He's getting fed up with waiting."

They climbed, with some difficulty, over a wide, low line of rocks that ran from the cliff right into the sea. Emily slipped on the wet rocks and her foot went into a tidepool. She stopped to shake her sneaker dry.

"How much farther do you think we'll have to go?" she asked, straining to see ahead of them. "The dog did come this way, didn't he? I haven't seen him for a while."

"I *think* he came over these rocks," Neil said. "He must have — unless he swam around."

There was a piercing whistle from Bob Parker, and Neil and Emily looked up to see their dad waving to them.

"I think Dad wants us to go back up," Emily said.

Neil nodded. "From where he is, he can probably see the sea coming in. When it does, it'll completely cover these rocks."

Out of sight, the dog howled again. Neil and Emily looked at each other.

"Let's just get to that high rock there and see if we can see over," Neil said, reluctant to give up.

They clambered across a little farther and, reaching a great sloping piece of black stone, leaned on it and peered over the top.

"This is it!" Neil said breathlessly. "This is Smugglers' Creek."

On the other side of the great stone wall, there was a tiny bay sheltered by towering cliffs. A passage between two rows of rocks led inward to a small, natural harbor that had been formed by continual erosion from the sea. Behind it was a dark, empty gash in the face of the cliff, cut off from them by the swelling tide.

"Look!" Neil pointed to the hole in the cliff face. "I bet that's the cave entrance!"

"Do you really think so?" Emily asked excitedly.

"Of course!" Neil said. "If this is Smugglers' Creek, then that must be the cave." His heart started to beat very fast. "This is where they sailed their boats at night and unloaded the stuff they'd stolen. They must have dragged it all up into the cave when the water was low enough. Can't you just see them, Em, sitting in the cave around a fire and sharing out their loot?"

Emily nodded, her eyes bright. "But how can we get in there?"

Neil shook his head. "It looks impossible. As Dad said, the whole layout of this bay must have changed over the years. You can't tell whether the sea goes out far enough now."

They stared at the scene in front of them, each deep in thought.

"Where's the dog?" Emily suddenly asked.

Neil shrugged. "Jeremiah Bones, where are you?" he shouted.

To their surprise, an answering howl came back. They looked at each other. The noise seemed to have come from the direction of the cave.

"That *was* just some sort of echo, wasn't it?" Emily said.

"I don't know," Neil said slowly. "But we've got to get out of here quickly before we get trapped. Come on!"

Neil was more convinced than ever that there was something strange and supernatural about the dog.

"I was beginning to get concerned," their mother said half an hour later, when Neil and Emily had climbed back up the cliff.

"You came back just in time — I was about to get the cliff rescue team out," Bob said, half joking.

"It was cool," Neil reassured him. "I was watching the tide all the time."

His mother raised her eyebrows. "Famous last words," she said wisely, as they moved away from the edge of the cliff.

Prunella yapped in Carole Parker's arms. She loved being carried and thought everybody should know it.

"If you come back to Mrs. Pendragon's with me,"

Neil said to his dad, "you can drop some hints about Prunes's diet."

Bob Parker gave a fake sigh. "No peace for the wicked!"

When they neared Prunella's cottage, Carole, Emily, and Sarah stayed back a little so as not to overwhelm the strange-looking woman, who was, as usual, looking out for her precious pooch to return.

Neil placed Prunella into her owner's arms, and then introduced his dad.

"Ah, so you're Mrs. Pendragon, and the lovely Prunella Pink's owner!" Bob said, smiling graciously.

"Oh, do call me Mildred," the woman beamed.

"And what a dog you've got!" Bob added.

While Mrs. Pendragon herself quivered with delight, Bob got in a few well-chosen words about the dog's diet and training. "Although I'm sure I don't need to tell you anything about dogs," he finished. "Something tells me you know all about the importance of regular exercise."

"Oh . . . of course!" Mrs. Pendragon said.

Neil coughed.

"Although I haven't been able to take her for many long walks lately," she added. "Too much to do in the garden."

"Sure," Bob Parker said. "But I know you'll keep up the good work from now on."

"Certainly," replied Mrs. Pendragon.

Neil promised to take Prunella on another walk
the following day. As he and his dad hurried to catch
up with the others, Neil glanced over at the dark
shape of the Penrose house between the trees. He
felt a sudden stab of regret. Although they'd found
the pirates' den, they weren't any closer to finding
out who the mysterious disappearing dachshund be-
longed to, or if Nicholas Penrose was really as guilty
of such a foul crime as local history said he was.

CHAPTER SEVEN

"**N**o, my name's *not* Penrose," Neil said patiently.

Emily rolled her eyes. "We're just here on vacation."

Neil and Emily were in Tregarth's old-fashioned candy store on the seafront. The couple in green overalls behind the counter had just gone through what had turned out to be the usual Tregarth routine on seeing Neil — first shock, then suspicion, ending in amazement.

"Can I *please* just buy some rock candy. It's a present," insisted Neil despairingly.

The couple hardly said a word as they wrapped up Neil's rock candy and took his money.

Neil and Emily were just turning to leave when the shop doorbell rang.

A tall man in a long dark raincoat came in. The man made his way to the counter, not looking to the left or right, and asked for something — so quietly that Neil couldn't hear what it was.

The woman behind the counter hurriedly served him as if she was eager to get the encounter over with.

The man said, "Thank you," in a low voice.

"Thank *you*, Mr. Penrose," the woman replied coolly.

Neil and Emily made amazed faces at each other and scurried outside.

"It's Mr. Penrose!" said Neil excitedly. "Victor Penrose!"

"In person!" said Emily.

"But they were so rude to him!" Neil said, shocked.

Sam stood up and rubbed his nose against Neil's leg.

"Good boy for waiting," Neil said absently, scratching Sam's ears and trying to see through the shop window. "What should we do?"

"About what?"

"Well, should we follow Mr. Penrose home or something?"

Emily's eyes widened. "We should talk to him."

At that moment, while they were still deciding what to do, Victor Penrose came out of the shop. He looked at Sam and a half smile crossed his face.

Then he saw Neil and stopped dead.

"It's OK," Neil spoke quickly, "I know I look like someone in your family."

The old man had turned pale. "Nicholas . . ." he faltered.

"Sorry to give you a shock," Neil said. "I'm Neil Parker and this is my sister Emily."

"We're staying at Summerbreeze," said Emily.

"This is our dog, Sam," said Neil, trying to get a regular conversation going.

Victor Penrose put out his hand. Once Sam had sniffed and accepted it, he patted him on the head, murmuring, "Good boy."

As Sam moved closer to the man, Neil relaxed.

"Have you got a dog?" asked Emily.

Victor Penrose nodded.

Neil's heart jumped.

Emily nudged him and Neil knew she was thinking the same thing. He decided to come straight out with it. "Is it a dachshund?" he asked boldly.

The old man paled again and looked at him in amazement. "Why do you ask that?"

"Oh, well . . . er . . ." Neil struggled. He didn't know what to say. How could he begin to explain about his mysterious dog friend?

The old man smiled faintly at him. "It's a very elderly German shepherd," he said. "Just like me. His name is Ellery and I've had him for fourteen years."

Emily nodded. "They're great, aren't they? Our parents run a boarding kennel, and we often have German shepherds visiting."

Victor Penrose smiled again, touched his hat, and began to move away.

"We're really pleased to have met you," said Neil quickly. "Can we walk with you up the hill? We'd really like to talk."

By the time they had arrived at the top of the hill and the gray stone wall that ran all around Mr. Penrose's house, Neil and Emily had told Victor Penrose everything about their trip so far. Neil had described his adventure after dark on their first night at Summerbreeze and about their investigations into the history of Black Saturday.

"Have *you* ever seen the dachshund?" Neil asked earnestly.

Mr. Penrose shook his head. He still looked rather shocked, as if he couldn't take in everything that was going on.

"I've never seen him, but I've heard him," said Mr. Penrose slowly. "Do you know there's a story about my house being haunted by Jeremiah Bones?"

"Really?" asked Neil.

"Well," said the old man, "they do say that the ghost of Jeremiah Bones still walks. He hasn't been seen for some years now, but my old aunt told me that she'd often seen him on the wharf waiting for the *Dark Lady* to come back. She sometimes saw him around the house, too — padding around, looking for Nicholas."

"A ghost dog," said Emily with a shiver.

"That's really sad," Neil said. Sam came closer and buried his nose in Neil's hand, as if to comfort him.

"Sometimes on stormy nights I think I hear him howling," Victor Penrose went on. "It's as if he wants something . . . someone to help him."

As they reached the gates of Penrose Manor, Neil turned to face the old man. "Look, I know this sounds crazy," he said, "but I feel that *someone* is *me*. I've got the weirdest feeling that maybe your ancestor — Nicholas — *wasn't* as wicked as everyone says he was."

Mr. Penrose's eyes looked sad. "I've always wondered about that, too. I mean, he was just a boy who, in the heat of the moment, ran away. I'm sure he would have come back. It was unfortunate that he was found by a pirate from the *Dark Lady* who was looking for a cabin boy."

Neil raised his eyebrows. "That's a different story from the one the museum curator told us."

"I expect it is," Mr. Penrose said. He looked admiringly at Sam sitting by Neil, waiting patiently for him to move on. "What a fine dog you've got there."

"He's the best," Neil said. "Look, we're only down

here until Sunday. Would it be possible for us to come and see you and maybe look around the house? I don't know if I can do anything to help, but maybe I'll find out when I get there."

"You're most welcome," Mr. Penrose said warmly, "although I doubt if anything could happen to clear the Penrose name after all these years."

Neil shrugged. "You never know."

"But maybe your father could do me a great favor, anyway — if he visits with you."

"What's that?" Neil asked.

"Ellery needs his nails clipped. The nearest vet is in the next village and since I no longer drive, I can't get there very easily."

Neil nodded. "I'll ask him."

"Will he have the necessary tools?"

"He always travels with a few basics," Emily said. "Just in case he gets asked to do something."

Mr. Penrose patted Sam, and said good-bye. "I'm most grateful to you," he added.

Neil smiled. "We haven't done anything yet."

"Just talking to someone has cheered me immensely," said Victor Penrose. "I feel better than I have in years."

As they walked away, Emily had a lump in her throat. "Poor old man," she said. "How come everyone in the village is so horrible to him?"

"I don't know," said Neil. But before he could say

more, there came from the direction of the beach a dog's sad howl.

Neil looked at Emily. "I am going to do something to help!" he said with determination. "I don't know what it is, but I'm going to do *something*!"

CHAPTER EIGHT

"**W**hat a beautiful house!" Carole Parker exclaimed as the family walked up the gravel driveway toward the stately gray building that was Penrose Manor. "Just imagine it in the olden days — with horse-drawn carriages outside and women in long dresses standing on the steps!"

Instead, on the steps outside the huge, shiny black doors, stood Victor Penrose with Ellery, his German shepherd. Ellery looked old but was still alert, with a sparkle in his eye that said he enjoyed having visitors — especially dog ones. Ellery padded down the steps slowly to greet Sam and both dogs circled each other cautiously for a moment, sniffing each other, then they touched noses. Seeming to like what they sniffed, they sat down together on the steps.

Victor Penrose smiled as he greeted the Parker family. "Welcome to my house."

Mr. Penrose shook hands with Bob and Carole.

The small party went through to the back kitchen where Mr. Penrose said he spent most of his time.

"All these rooms are too much for me now," he said as he led them through the vast hall with its rows of family portraits and suits of armor. "Six bedrooms with only me to sleep in them!"

"Do you have family living in other parts of the country?" Carole asked.

Mr. Penrose nodded. "Two sisters still living and lots of cousins. They all find life in these parts too difficult." His voice fell. "The locals never seem to forget."

"Er . . . was Nicholas a cousin of yours?" asked Emily.

"He would have been my uncle," Mr. Penrose said. "His younger brother Edward married a girl from Exeter and they came back to live in the house. They subsequently had me — and five other children — but the others moved away as soon as they could."

They reached the big, lofty kitchen with a long pine table, and went through to another, smaller, room that Mr. Penrose called the scullery.

"Let's check you out, shall we, boy?" Bob said to Ellery soothingly, positioning the dog near the sink. "Could you hold his paw for me, Neil?"

Neil had helped his dad perform this task several times before, so he knew just what to do. Bob steadied the dog, took out a pair of steel clippers, and, before Ellery even knew what was happening, carefully snipped the long, hard nails that had been preventing him from running around as much as he would have liked.

This small operation finished, the family was invited to look around the house. This was just what Neil and Emily had been waiting for. . . .

"Well, I see what you mean!" Carole Parker said in amazement, looking at the portrait in front of her.

Back in the marble-floored hall, Carole, Neil,

Emily, and Sarah had just come across another portrait of young Nicholas Penrose, sitting in a leather armchair in the library of the house. By his side, looking up at him devotedly, was the faithful dachshund, Jeremiah Bones. Nicholas's hand was resting affectionately on his dog's head.

"The likeness between you and this Nicholas Penrose is remarkable," Carole gasped. "No wonder everyone is spooked when they meet you."

"Sam! Look at Neil!" Sarah said, trying to get the dog to look at the portrait. At the mention of his name, the dog looked at the real Neil.

"No. The one in the picture!" Sarah said, pointing at the oil painting.

"*That's* the dog Neil and I have been seeing around the place," Emily said to her mother, pointing to Jeremiah Bones in the portrait.

"It's a beautiful house," Carole Parker said, changing the subject as she marveled at the vast curved oak staircase. "But it's in pretty bad shape now," she added in a low voice.

Emily turned away from the painting and tugged Neil's sleeve. "What are we supposed to be looking for?"

"I don't know," he said. "Clues, I suppose."

They hadn't found a thing so far. Mr. Penrose had showed them the upper floors, including Nicholas's actual bedroom. The room looked like it hadn't been touched since Nicholas left, but there were no obvious clues to his fate. Neil and Emily had both been disappointed.

The other rooms were filled with old, bulky wooden furniture, most of which was covered in white sheets. As they peeped into each room the dust, disturbed by the opening of the door, rose and swirled.

Neil went and stood in the bay window of the grand front room, with its doors leading onto a long paved terrace. He was thinking about Nicholas. Had he stood here, at this very window, looking down the hill and toward the sea? What sort of boy was he? Had he just gone looking for adventure and somehow gotten mixed up with the wrong crowd? Or were the villagers right: Was he a wicked person who cared for nothing but doing evil for evil's sake? No, Neil didn't think so.

Beside him, Carole shook her head. "It's all very sad. Victor Penrose seems like such a nice old man."

Neil sighed. "I want to find out what happened to Nicholas and clear the Penrose name."

His mother put her hand on his shoulder. "I know, Neil. But I think the best we *can* do is to be nice and friendly to Mr. Penrose while we're here. He's obviously a very lonely person."

Sam, who'd been sniffing around the room investigating interesting mousy smells, suddenly barked.

"What's up, Sam?" Neil asked.

"He sensed something," Emily said, and she and

Neil went to the side window of the room, where Sam had been nosing about.

"It's Jeremiah Bones!" Neil said excitedly. "Come on, Em, let's go out there and see what he wants!"

Neil ran over to the tall glass doors that led onto the outside terrace, but they were bolted at the top.

"Quickly! Before he disappears again," said Emily.

"Careful, you two," said Carole.

Reaching up, Neil slid open the bolt, and he, Emily, and Sam dashed down the stone steps and across the grass.

Emily stopped dead. "Where's he gone now?"

"Behind those bushes?" Neil suggested, pointing.

Some distance from the house, in the center of the lawn, there was a circle of shrubs and small trees, some green and others an autumnal gold. While Sam took off in the opposite direction to investigate some marble statues, Neil and Emily made their way toward the circle.

Pushing into the middle of it, Neil saw the shadow of a dog flicker on the leaves of a bush and its branches quiver slightly as someone passed.

"Over there!" he pointed. "I saw something. . . . I don't know what."

But Emily was standing, transfixed, in the center of the circle. "You know what this is, don't you?" she said to her brother in a low voice.

A chill ran up the back of Neil's neck. Somehow, he *did* know. "It's a pet cemetery," he said, for the rough circle was formed by ten or so shrubs, and beside each of these was a small tombstone.

"Oh, look. *Binkie. 1848–1862. Beloved pet of Victoria Penrose and an excellent mouser*," Emily read out. She moved along a little. "And this one: *Rufus. 1860–1872. The Penrose family hunting hound and the best dog of all*."

"*Sebastian. 1901–1905. You stayed such a little while*," Neil said, almost whispering.

"Oh, my," Emily sniffed, and fumbled in her pocket to see if she had a tissue.

Neil suddenly caught hold of Emily's arm and nodded toward where he'd seen the glimmer of movement. "Over there!"

They made their way to a golden-leaved bush. Beside it, rather lopsided in the ground, was a small gray tombstone.

"*The good Jeremiah Bones, 1892–1908. Faithful even after death. Awaiting his master's return*," Neil read out.

"He led us here!" Emily said. "But *why* . . . ?"

They both stared at the writing on the stone. "Maybe he just wanted us to know that we were on the right track," Neil said.

His sister nodded.

"It *is* a ghost we've been seeing," Neil said intently.

Emily nodded again. "The ghost of Jeremiah Bones," she said in an awestruck voice.

"But what is it we have to do?" Neil sighed. "What

The good
Jeremiah
Bones
1892 ~ 1908
faithful even
after death.
Awaiting his
master's
return

is it he wants us to find? We're only here until Sunday."

"I know," Emily said. "And it's already Friday."

"We don't seem to be any closer to solving things! Do you believe me now — about Nicholas Penrose not being as wicked as they say he was?"

Emily gave the question some consideration. "I suppose I do," she said after a moment. "I mean, there must be a reason why all these things have happened, and why Jeremiah Bones keeps turning up."

"Faithful even after death," Neil said almost to himself. "Do you think that means the dog was faithful after Nicholas's death, or that he was faithful even after he died himself?"

"What do you mean?" Emily said, struggling to understand.

"Well, was Jeremiah Bones so faithful that even when he was dead, he came back to try and help his master?"

Emily scrunched up her face. "I don't know," she said.

There was a sudden piercing whistle from the direction of the house and Neil and Emily looked toward it. On the terrace steps stood Bob Parker with old Victor Penrose and Ellery.

"Come on, you two!" their father called. "We're having a snack in the kitchen now."

Sam was already racing across the lawn toward the house in response to the whistle as, rather reluctantly, Neil and Emily left the pet cemetery and made their way back.

"How's Ellery now?" Neil asked when they reached the house.

"Running around quite nimbly for an old boy," Bob Parker said.

"A bit like me!" said Mr. Penrose, and Neil thought he was looking much more cheerful than the downcast figure they'd spoken to outside the candy store the day before.

Bob patted the sturdy German shepherd beside him. "He'll find it easier to get around now."

Sam positioned himself respectfully, one step below Ellery. Bob laughed. "He knows his place," he said.

"We found the pet cemetery," Neil said to Mr. Penrose as they all went indoors.

"Ah, yes," Mr. Penrose said. He smiled rather sadly. "There are a lot of well-loved pets buried there. This family has always loved animals."

"And we saw Jeremiah Bones's grave, as well," Emily put in.

Mr. Penrose nodded.

"We think we saw him, too!" Neil said.

His dad clapped him on the back. "Come on, Neil, none of your weird and wonderful stories now. Mr. Penrose has made us a snack. Let's go and enjoy it!"

Neil sighed. "One more day . . ." he said almost to himself. "I've only got one more day to clear the name of Nicholas Penrose."

CHAPTER NINE

At the first howl from outside his window, Neil was awake. It was Jeremiah Bones again!

He lay there in the soft darkness of the bedroom for a few moments, listening to the sad howling and wondering if it was going to go on all night. What could he do? What did the dog *want*?

The howling continued. Jeremiah Bones, don't you ever give up? Neil thought.

And then he had another thought, one which made a shiver run right down his spine in spite of the thick blankets on the bed. He sat up, reached under the bed for his flashlight, and switched it on.

"What's that?" Emily murmured in her sleep, and turned over.

"I've just got to check something," Neil said excitedly, scrambling onto the floor. By the bed was the little collection of information they'd gathered about Black Saturday — mostly photocopies from newspapers and books from Tregarth library.

Neil flipped through the sheets hurriedly. "Yes!" he crowed, and then he remembered to lower his voice. "Emily!" he hissed. "Em, you've got to wake up." He got out of bed and shook his sister. "Guess what?"

"What?" Emily groaned. "What time is it? It's the middle of the night!"

"Today's the day. Black Saturday!"

"What are you talking about?"

"Today is Saturday, October twentieth. Exactly one hundred years ago today it was Black Saturday!"

Emily propped herself up on one elbow. "Really?" she asked sleepily.

"It has to mean something, doesn't it?"

"I suppose so."

"And can you hear Jeremiah Bones howling?"

Emily nodded, pushing her dark hair out of her eyes.

"He's waiting for us, Em. We've got to go out there and follow him!"

Emily slid down the bed slightly. "What, now? Right this minute? Do we have to?" she pleaded. "It's so cold and dark."

"Of course we have to!" Neil said urgently. "This is our big chance."

"If you say so . . ." she replied, pushing back the bedding and fumbling for her socks.

Fifteen minutes later Neil and Emily, together with Sam, were making their way along the top of the cliffs behind the dachshund, Jeremiah Bones. A salty wind was blowing in from the sea and, in spite of wearing practically every piece of clothing they'd brought with them, Emily and Neil were still cold. Sam ran ahead of them, his breath clouding up in frosty puffs. Every so often he would run back to Neil, very excited to be going for a walk in the middle of the night.

"I'm glad I've got this flashlight," Neil said. Although there was a full moon, it kept going behind clouds, throwing their path into darkness.

They continued along the cliff, getting glimpses of the vast, silky black sea whenever the moon came out. As before, Jeremiah Bones seemed to disappear as they neared Zennor Point.

Emily sighed. "Don't tell me we've got to go down that little path again."

Neil nodded. "I'm afraid so. You know where Jeremiah is leading us, don't you?"

"Smugglers' Creek again?" Emily said.

"That's right. I know it's a bit tricky, but at least we've already done it in daylight. And if the sky stays clear I think we'll be able to see OK."

With the light from the flashlight, Neil searched

for the small path down to the beach that they'd taken a few days previously. "It'll be all right," he urged Emily. "We'll be down there in no time at all."

"If you say so," Emily said, hugging her arms around her to keep warm. "What about Sam, though? Is he coming down as well?"

"We can't leave him here," Neil said, calling him to come over. "If we take it slowly and steadily, he'll be fine. He's very surefooted."

There was a long howl from the beach far below them. "There's Jeremiah Bones, right on cue!" Neil said.

Emily took a deep breath. "Should I go first?"

As they set off, the moon came out fully, shining on the cliff and reflecting light off the water, making it much easier to choose the safest footholds.

"Easy!" Neil said when they reached the sand. "We could have done it with our eyes closed!"

As Sam pranced around, kicking up sand, investigating smells, Neil looked out to sea. "The tide's miles out."

"Yeah, but remember what Dad said about it turning quickly," Emily reminded him.

Neil nodded. "We'd better get going."

As if he'd heard him, Jeremiah Bones suddenly appeared ahead of them, silhouetted against the sky on top of a rock.

"Come on, Em. It's now or never!" said Neil.

They walked across the beach, past the wreck, until the sand turned to shingle, then stones, and then disappeared altogether. They began clambering over the slippery rocks.

Jeremiah Bones was still in front of them, always a short distance ahead, but Neil thought he didn't seem nearly so jumpy or impatient. Whenever they stopped to catch their breath he would just sit quietly, waiting for them to start off again.

"He's different. It's as if he knows that it was all leading up to tonight," Neil said.

"Well, I hope you're right," Emily said. "I'd hate to think I was rock climbing in the middle of the night for nothing!"

Going on, they reached the last huge wedge of dark granite they'd leaned on before, with Smugglers' Creek on the other side. Jeremiah Bones was already over, howling for them to join him.

"And how are we supposed to get over this?" Emily asked, slapping the cold rock with her bare hand.

Neil considered. "Well, we'll get on one of the footholds and lift Sam up first, then I'll give you a heave over and then you pull me up." He tucked the flashlight inside his sweater for safety. "Come on, let's go!"

Somehow, they managed it, and slid down onto the rock. The sea was closer here, crashing against the outer rocks of the harbor and echoing back to the cliff walls. The moon was fully out and low in the sky, shining eerily on the water and making it gleam silver.

Sam began to run down the rocks, which led toward the sea, barking with excitement. Neil had to whistle for him to come back. He did so, looking longingly out to the sea as if he'd just love to have a swim.

"You wouldn't want to go in there, Sam!" Neil said, scratching his ears. "It's absolutely freezing."

Emily suddenly bit her lip and moaned. "I just thought of something, Neil. Suppose Mom or Dad wakes up and see that we're gone? We should have left them a note."

"Saying what? *Won't be long, have gone down dangerous cliff path in darkness . . .*"

". . . *following ghost dog,*" Emily finished. "OK. Maybe not."

Neil looked for Jeremiah Bones and saw him sitting on a rock. Then he noticed something startling. "Look at the cave!" he said.

Emily looked. Where the sea had lapped at the cave's entrance, now there was only rock and sand. "If we're careful, we can climb around that far," she said.

"Exactly," Neil said. "And that means we can get in there!"

Emily gave a shudder. "Is it safe to go in, though? I mean, how do we know that when we get inside we won't get cut off by the sea?"

"Well, I . . ." Neil said, and then shrugged. "It's low tide now but I don't know when it's going to turn. We've just got to trust Jeremiah Bones."

"Trust a dog that probably doesn't exist?"

"We'll be all right," Neil said, remembering Nicholas Penrose in his dream. "We've got to trust him."

As they entered the cave behind the dog, Neil was more grateful than ever for the flashlight. He patted his side for Sam to come. Neil realized there might be passages leading from the main cave, and the last thing he wanted was for Sam to wander off on his own.

Emily looked behind them. "I wish we could tie a

piece of string to the entrance and unravel it as we go, just to make sure we can find our way out again."

"We can follow our footprints back," Neil said, looking down. The sand inside the cave was damp beneath their feet. Where they'd walked, there were the clear imprints of two pairs of shoes. *And one set of dog's paws.*

As Emily looked, her jaw dropped. "Two of us, but only one dog!"

"I suppose ghosts don't make tracks," Neil said.

Emily stared at the footprints in amazement. "No one will ever believe this, Neil! They'll think we're crazy. If we tell *any* of this to anyone at school, our lives won't be worth living for weeks."

There was a short bark from Jeremiah Bones ahead of them in the dark, and Neil shone the flashlight's beam in front of them. "I'll go first." He patted his leg. "Stay by, Sam," he said as they set off.

As they walked farther into the cave, Neil sniffed the air and made a face. "Seawater, fish, and seaweed. What a lovely smell. *Not!*"

Ahead of them, Jeremiah Bones barked again and Emily shivered. "A ghost dog is one thing, but I hope there aren't any ghost pirates hanging around," she said fearfully.

As they walked, Neil shone his flashlight up and down the walls of the cave, which were running with water.

A short bark came from very close by, making

them jump. Neil pointed his flashlight ahead and was surprised to find that they'd almost come to a dead end. "What now?" he said. "This is as far as the cave goes."

"But we haven't found anything! And where's Jeremiah Bones?"

Ahead of them, the rock ceiling of the cave dipped right down, almost meeting the rocks of the floor and forming a rough shelf that ran around the edge of the semicircular space.

"I bet the pirates used to hold their meetings here," Emily said, staring ahead. "I bet they used to sit here and share their treasure."

"Maybe," Neil said absently, wondering what he should do next.

From the farthermost, darkest corner came another bark from the dachshund. Sam quivered all over and gave an uneasy whine.

Neil took a step toward where the bark came from.

He saw Jeremiah Bones come out of the shadows, and leap from the ground toward a half-hidden rocky shelf.

As if in a dream, Neil walked toward the shelf near where the dog was standing and put out his hand. Instead of just touching rock, he touched something else. Carefully, he lifted it out.

"What's that?" Emily asked excitedly.

"Some sort of . . . packet," Neil said, turning it over in his hands.

"Let me look!" Emily said. "Is it treasure?"

"No. I think it's an old pouch. It's made of something . . . oily. It looks waterproof. I think it's got something inside. And I can see the words . . ." Neil opened the top of the pouch and moved the flashlight's beam over it. "Nicholas Penrose!"

As Emily's mouth dropped open in astonishment, there was a tremendous crash as the first wave of the incoming tide thundered back into the cave. Sam let out a bark of alarm.

"Quickly!" Neil said. "The tide's turned. We've got to get out!"

"Is there anything else there?" Emily asked urgently.

Neil ran his hand along the shelf. "Nothing at all."

"Where's Jeremiah Bones?" asked Emily, urgently looking around.

"He's vanished," replied Neil incredulously.

As the waves crashed again more loudly, Neil

tucked the precious packet safely underneath his sweater.

"Come on," he said, grabbing his sister's hand. "Lead the way out, Sam!"

The three of them ran back through the cave as fast as they could.

CHAPTER TEN

"**W**e got a little wet running out of the cave," Neil said to his mom and dad, "but only our feet."

"And then we climbed up over the rocks, ran along the beach, up the path . . ."

"And came home!" Neil finished, as if he was talking about a trip to the local shops. "It was no big deal. We were never in any danger," he added sheepishly. "But Jeremiah disappeared completely."

When Neil and Emily had burst into Summerbreeze, they'd been far too excited to keep the news of what had happened to themselves. While Emily had gone to find warm socks for both of them, Neil had gone to wake up his mom and dad. And now, while dawn was breaking over the small village and Sarah was still sleeping upstairs, they were downstairs in the kitchen, drinking cocoa and recounting the details of their latest, dramatic shoreline exploration.

"I don't know what to say," Carole Parker said, shaking her head. "It just wasn't smart of you to go out in the middle of the night."

"Especially without leaving a note!" Bob Parker said. "And such an extraordinary story. Ghost dog indeed!" He shook his head. "I must say I can't really understand what's going on here."

"If I'd woken up in the morning and found you missing, I'd have had a fit!" Carole said. "Don't you ever do that again!"

"What — go out after a ghost dog and follow him into a pirates' cave?" Neil said, grinning. "No, I can safely say I won't be doing that back home."

"And what about Sam?" asked Bob Parker, bending to pat Sam under the table. "What made you think he'd like to go trekking across beaches in the middle of the night?"

Sam thumped his tail on the floor at the mention of his name. Everyone knew he'd enjoyed every minute of his outing — including the short swim at the end!

"Come *on*, Neil!" Emily said impatiently. "Let's see what we've found."

"Yes, let's see what you've risked life and limb for," Bob said.

As Neil took the old pouch out from inside his

sweater, he drew in his breath, closed his eyes, and wished. Everything hung on this. If, after all that had happened, it was just some old meaningless piece of writing, he didn't know what he'd do.

Slowly, he opened the flap and eased out a piece of parchment.

"At the top it says, *Nicholas Penrose. His true words*," Neil read, "and the date."

He moved the paper into the light in order to see it better. "It's written funny," he said, "and it's a bit smudged and blotted, but I think I can read it OK."

With fingers that were shaking a little with excitement, he began to read.

"I, Nicholas Penrose, know that these will be my final words. I do not write to absolve myself from my past doings, but so those who come after will know that I was not entirely bad.

"I, together with my loyal Jeremiah Bones, joined a band of men this past summer, not thinking about what it would lead to. At first I was ignorant of their ways, and thought them a merry group. I acted as cabin boy and because of my wealthy connections, I was able to tell them many secrets, which helped their thieving trade. I am ashamed to say that I thought little of what my conduct was doing to my family.

"Only as the weeks passed did I become aware of the evil and vile nature of this band of men I had undertaken to live with. And tonight, this twentieth of October, when they made clear their intention to rob, plunder, and ransack my home village, I begged them not to go; I begged that I be released from my duties. Alas, they would not listen to me. It seems that all these months they have been taking me for a fool, and using me to gain access to village secrets.

"And now they have foot-chained me to a rock here in the cave, and intend to torture out of me my further knowledge of moneyed people when they return. Then I am to be killed."

Around the table, Bob, Carole, and Emily held their breath, completely engrossed.

Neil continued. *"To try and lessen the harm on the people of Tregarth, I have written a note of warning and sent it into the village with my good dog, Jeremiah Bones. I pray that the people will not turn him away, but read the note and prepare to defend themselves.*

"May my family know of my sorrow for the shame I brought upon them, and also know that I did all I could to stop this evil. These are the last words I shall ever write. May someone look after my faithful Jeremiah until he can be reunited with his loving master, Nicholas Penrose, after death."

As Neil stared at the parchment, the family was silent; each had their own private thoughts.

A moment later, Carole Parker shook her head sadly. "Poor boy," she said.

"Yeah," Neil said shakily, feeling under the table to ruffle Sam's fur. "Poor Nicholas — and poor Jeremiah Bones."

Bob Parker blew his nose loudly. "Well," he said, "I don't understand how you've managed to get hold of this information, but we've been given it for a reason and we'd better use it. We'll go over to see Victor Penrose right after breakfast!"

Neil and Emily let out huge sighs of relief and smiled.

It was just after ten o'clock when the little party set off from Summerbreeze toward the house of Victor

Penrose. As they passed Mrs. Pendragon's cottage, the eccentric woman came outside with the fat Yorkshire terrier under her arm. When she saw Bob, she hastily put the little dog down. "We're just off to the village," she piped up cheerily. "Prunella Pink was going to walk, of course."

"It's a lovely morning for a walk!" Bob Parker said. He bent down to pat Prunella. "Have you tried the dog biscuits I recommended?" he asked.

She nodded and blushed. "Of course," she said. "I always take the advice of an expert."

Neil looked at Prunella closely. Although she still had the pink bow in her hair, Neil thought that he could detect a difference in her health. She looked perkier, her eyes shone brightly, her nose glistened — and she was definitely a little narrower around the middle. "Hello, Prunes!" he said. "Coming for a last walk with us? Up to see Mr. Penrose?"

Mrs. Pendragon's face darkened. "Oh. You're going up there, are you?"

"Victor Penrose is actually a very nice man, Mrs. Pendragon," said Bob Parker gently. "And his family's poor reputation is much exaggerated."

"What do you mean?"

"I mean my kids here have discovered something . . . some paperwork relating to what I believe is known here as Black Saturday."

"I don't understand," Mrs. Pendragon said in confusion, her silk scarves flying around her. "What is it? How did they come by it?"

"I'm sorry, but we'd like to tell Mr. Penrose first," Neil interrupted.

"Although I'm sure it'll be all over the village by this afternoon," Carole said. "It really is very exciting."

"Well!" said Mrs. Pendragon, clearly astounded.

"We'll come back and tell you later!" Emily said, feeling a bit sorry for her.

"Bye, Prunes!" chorused Neil and Emily as they left Mrs. Pendragon wondering what was going on.

"Poor, poor Nicholas," said Victor Penrose shakily, when, with many interruptions from Emily, Neil had finished recounting the story. "To think he died in the cave that very night, at the hands of those barbarians. He didn't go away with them."

"It's very sad," Carole said softly. "He was so young, too."

"And everyone believed he'd betrayed this village." Victor Penrose suddenly got up from the heavy wooden table in the kitchen that everyone was sitting around. "Of course! Oh, of course!" he said suddenly.

The Parkers looked at him expectantly.

"*The note!* The note he said he sent with Jeremiah Bones!"

"What about it?" Neil asked.

"Had you heard about it before?" said Emily.

"Not only that . . ." Mr. Penrose said. He went to the door and beckoned to them. "Come into the library. I want to show you something. I think you'll find it most illuminating."

He led the family through the house, with Sam and Ellery bringing up the rear, pushed open the door of the library, and went in. "I've told you the family story about the ghost of Jeremiah Bones. Well, I just remembered something else."

As Neil and Emily looked at each other excitedly, Victor Penrose went over to a small shelf of books in an alcove, and picked out a thin red leather volume. "There's something that has been kept in here through the years, but no one has ever worked out what it actually was."

He opened the book and took out a small piece of paper, very crumpled and brown at the edges. "My aunt told me that on Black Saturday, Jeremiah Bones was found in a distressed state on the cliffs above Smugglers' Creek. Someone told her later that the dog had tried to go into Tregarth but the villagers, knowing him to be Nicholas's dog — Nicholas who was with the wicked pirates — had turned him away. Someone had even thrown a stone at him."

"That's terrible!" Neil said, outraged.

"Apparently, Jeremiah tried several times to approach people, but no one would have anything to do with him. Some days later he came back here and we found this piece of parchment underneath his collar, twisted around and around to keep it safe. It had gotten wet and was practically unreadable by then . . ."

"Can we see?" Neil asked, and Mr. Penrose brought the parchment over to him.

"It's the same writing! I'm sure it's Nicholas's writing!"

"I can just make out the words *danger* and *de-*

fend," Carole said, looking over Neil's shoulder. "Nothing else, though."

"So although everyone believed Nicholas had betrayed the village, really he'd tried to save it," Mr. Penrose said with a sigh. "*This* is the note he referred to in his letter."

His gnarled old hands smoothed out the note. "Now, what should we do first?"

"We thought you might want to take the letter down to the museum," said Emily.

"Oh, I will," said the old man. "And I'll take this note, too. But first I'm going to call the local newspaper and get them over here to hear the full story. This will be big news around these parts."

"How exciting!" Sarah said, beaming. "Will they want to take our photograph?"

"I'm sure they will," Victor Penrose said. "The Penrose family have made the headlines several times in the past, but have always been shown in a most unfavorable light. Now, at last, I'll be able to tell the true story." He smiled at Neil and Emily. "You've done this family a wonderful service by clearing our name, and I'll always be grateful."

"That's OK," Neil said, grinning. "We enjoyed it. And anyway, it wasn't just us. Mostly it was Jeremiah Bones." He called Sam over to him and buried his face in his fur. "Dogs are brilliant, aren't they?"

"They are!" said Mr. Penrose, looking fondly at

Ellery. "And the good Jeremiah Bones is perhaps the most brilliant of all."

Sarah, who'd wandered into the hall of Penrose Manor and had been playing with Sam, suddenly ran into the kitchen. "The dog's in the garden!" she cried.

"What dog?" Carole asked. "Prunella?"

"No. The Jermy Bones dog," Sarah said. "He's by the trees."

Neil and Emily were first out of the room. They ran through the hall to a window at the back of the house.

"Yes, there he is!" Emily pointed. She lowered her voice because of Sarah. "Just outside the pet cemetery."

"He's right by where he's buried," Neil said. "And he looks . . . different."

"He looks happy!" Sarah said.

"That's it!" Neil said. "He's wagging his tail. He's done what he set out to do."

"He's leaving!" Emily said. "Look, Neil. He's going into those bushes!"

Neil was silent as he watched the leaves and branches obscure the dog completely.

By the time his parents and Mr. Penrose got to the window, the dog had gone and the leaves on the bushes had settled back into place.

"Well, I can't see him!" Bob Parker said, peering over the grass.

"And neither can I," said Carole.

"No, he's gone now," said Neil. "Jeremiah Bones has gone."

"Gone forever," said Emily. "I think he deserves a good rest."

"Yeah, that's right, Em. The dog served his master faithfully," he said, "but now his job's over. I'm happy we were able to reunite him with his master."

Bob Parker coughed gently. "Come on, everybody. It's time to go back home now. Back to King Street Kennels."

Neil and Emily walked away from the pet cemetery slowly. Emily sighed. "Thank you for letting us help you, Jeremiah Bones."